Illustrated by

D1352282

013958192 X

With special thanks to:

Everyone at Renaissance Learning
and to:

Chris, Heather and everyone at
Scottish Book Trust
for their continued support.

First published in 2010 in Great Britain by
Barrington Stoke Ltd
18 Walker St, Edinburgh, EH3 7LP

www.barringtonstoke.co.uk

This edition published 2012

ISBN: 978-1-78112-040-8

Printed in China by Leo

Contents

Chapter 1
Stand Up and Be Counted

"Mr Miller ..." the teacher began. He was talking to me. I'm Matthew Miller and I hadn't been at the school that long.

No, don't do this. Please ... I begged him in my head.

"... would you stand up for me?" the teacher went on.

Please, no! That voice in my head was getting louder.

My chair made a horrible scratching noise across the floor as I stood up. Everyone in class turned to look at me – the kids who'd said hello to me once or twice, the kids who looked at me as if I wasn't there, and the bully who'd already begun to pick on me. Neil was the only real friend I'd made. He made a weird face because we both knew what was about to happen. He did that a lot when he was worried.

"How long have you been at Elm Road School, now, Mr Miller?" The teacher's voice rang out around the classroom.

"Three weeks, sir," I answered. I was trying to keep my voice from cracking.

"And, in that time, have you noticed anything different about yourself when you look at the other people in the school?"

I heard a noise. A sort of snigger and snort. I didn't need to look round to see who'd made it – there was only one person who made a sound like that. It was Steven Chadwick. He was the bully who thought it was fun to make me his new victim.

"I don't know what you mean, sir," I said. My voice began to shake that time.

"Let me make it easy, Mr Miller ..." said the teacher. His name was Mr Smith – he was my History teacher. He always called people by their last names as if he was meeting them for the first time. He'd never called me Matthew.

"If you look around the class," Mr Smith went on, "you'll see that everyone is dressed the same. They're all wearing black trousers, white shirts, grey jumpers and yellow and blue ties. In other words, Mr Miller, everyone is wearing correct school uniform. Everyone, but you."

I felt my cheeks begin to burn. I'd been waiting for this moment and worrying about it. Now it was happening, it was even worse than I'd thought.

"You, Mr Miller, are wearing jeans and a T-shirt. Don't the school rules apply to you?" Mr Smith grinned.

"Yes, sir," I squeaked. Steven Chadwick laughed out loud.

Mr Smith wasn't going to stop. "Then can you tell me why, after three weeks at Elm Road School, you are still not wearing the correct uniform?"

I heard Neil turning about in his seat. I wanted to look down at him and see a friendly face but I couldn't move. It was as if I was frozen with embarrassment.

"My mum ..." I began. I had to fight back the burning feeling in my eyes. I wasn't going to cry. No way. Not in front of Steven Chadwick. "My mum can't afford to buy me a school uniform yet, sir."

About half the class giggled. *Please let that be the end of it,* I begged Mr Smith silently.

"Then what about your father, Mr Miller?" said the teacher. "Why can't you ask your father to get you one?"

This was like torture. Why was Mr Smith doing this to me?

"I don't know where my dad is, sir," I had to say. I gulped. Why did he have to bring my rubbish dad into it?

This time everyone giggled.

"Don't know where he is?" Mr Smith asked with a sneer.

"He ran off with the woman from two doors down to us, sir," I said. I might as well tell him everything now. "Then we couldn't afford to stay in our house, so we moved to a flat near here, sir. My mum has two jobs and sleeps on the couch so I can have the only bedroom, sir."

What else do you want? I looked hard at Mr Smith as the class began to whisper about me and my mum.

"OK, that's all, Matthew," said Mr Smith. He picked up some papers on his desk as I sat down. He didn't look at me any more.

But someone else was looking right at me. Steven Chadwick. He was grinning like all his birthdays had come at once.

Chapter 2
Big Brother

At lunch break Chadwick got me at last. He was prowling the playground as always. He had the two idiots who follow him everywhere with him. Their names are Ian Bates and Billy Wilson. Wilson spotted me first and prodded Chadwick in the ribs.

"Well, well ..." shouted Chadwick as he marched over to me. "I didn't know we let scum like you in this school!"

I felt myself start to go red again. Chadwick had been after me ever since I started at this school. Now the other kids in the playground stepped back so that the bullies could get me. They were just glad it wasn't their turn to be picked on yet. I didn't have to look at Neil – I knew he was nervous and that he was staring at me.

"Poor kids are no good to me," Chadwick sneered. He stopped and looked me up and down. "How can I nick your dinner money when you haven't got any?" Bates and Wilson snorted like this was the funniest joke in the world.

"I've got dinner money," I said softly. It wasn't true. I had enough money for a sandwich and that was about it, but I wasn't going to tell Chadwick that.

The bully put out his hand for it. "Give it here," he growled.

"No," I said and I put my hands in my pockets.

Chadwick grabbed my hair and pulled my head back. "I said, give it here!" he snarled. I heard Neil take a deep breath. Maybe he was going to stand up for me? But he didn't move. He turns to jelly every time he even sees the bullies.

Chadwick gripped my hair tighter. It felt like he was going to pull it out by the roots. "Now!" he barked. I pushed a hand into the pocket of my jeans and pulled out some coins. I threw them onto the ground. Bates and Wilson dropped down to pick up the money.

At last, Chadwick let go of my hair. "Same time tomorrow?" he grinned as he turned to walk away. His two pet monkeys – Bates and Wilson – ran after him. They were still counting my dinner money.

Everyone else in the playground stood still and stared at me like I was a big loser. But I bet they'd all had the same treatment at some point.

Neil and I walked home together at the end of the day.

"You need to stay far away from Steven Chadwick," said Neil. His mouth was full of chocolate.

"Thanks for that, Captain Obvious!" I said. I couldn't really complain because he'd bought some sweets on the way home and now he was sharing them with me. They made me feel a bit less starving.

"Still, we should be glad it's Steven Chadwick who had a go at you and not his big brother," added Neil.

"Who's his big brother?" I asked. I opened my second bag of crisps.

"Daniel Chadwick," Neil said. He looked round quickly to make sure no one else was there. "He murdered a teacher!" he whispered.

"Don't be stupid!" I laughed. I knew how stories like that started. There was a kid at my old school who'd broken a window in the science block. Before long, the story was that he'd demolished half the school.

"He did!" retorted Neil. "But he got away with it. They said it was 'manslaughter', and that he'd been pushed into it."

I could tell that Neil was telling the truth! "What happened?" I asked.

"There was this Maths teacher called Mr Taylor," Neil began. "He had Daniel Chadwick in one of his classes. Daniel Chadwick was a real hard case. He called himself 'Dan The Man'. He'd argue with teachers just for the hell of it. Anyway, somehow a fight started and Daniel pushed Mr Taylor over. He hit his head on a desk and died the next day in hospital."

We walked on. We were both very quiet. Well, I say quiet – but you could hear Neil chomping on his sweets a mile away. "What happened to Chadwick's brother?" I asked.

"He went to prison," said Neil. "Or some young offender's centre, anyway. Good thing, too. He was evil."

It didn't seem like this story could be real. "How come I've never heard about this before?" I said.

Neil gave a shrug. "No one really talks about it at school," he said. "Chadwick goes mental if anyone talks about Daniel going to prison, but I bet he'd do the exact same thing if he ever got into a fight with a teacher. He's evil, too." We were at the end of Neil's road now. "Right!" Neil said, "see you tomorrow!"

I was still thinking about Daniel Chadwick when I got home. I didn't even see that my mum was grinning. "Guess what I found in the charity shop?" she said and she held up a plastic carrier bag.

Chapter 3
The Uniform

The shirt was a little bit scruffy around the collar and cuffs but my mum soaked it and washed it and after that it looked and smelled clean. She had to take the trousers up a few inches. The person who'd owned them before me must have been a lot taller than me. They'd written 'DTM' on all the labels. With the shirt and jumper on, I looked just like every other boy at Elm Road School.

Neil grinned when he came to fetch me for school the next morning. He still looked babyish when he smiled, but it was better than his worried look.

"Hey!" he said. "You look cool!"

"I'm in exactly the same clothes as you!" I said and I shook my head. But he was right. I didn't look too bad at all.

We set off for school. "Maybe Chadwick will leave you alone now," he said.

"That just means he'll bully someone else," I said.

"So long as it's not you, don't worry about it!" smiled Neil.

We started to talk about football. It turned out that Neil and I both supported the same team. I told him about the times my dad had taken me to see them play at the home matches. One year, he even got us season tickets. Neil had never been to a real game, he only watched them on TV, but he said he'd ask his dad to take us the next time he wasn't at work on a Saturday.

For the ten minute walk to school, I felt like the old me again. Like none of the stuff with my dad had ever happened. So what if I was living in a crappy little flat and had a second-hand school uniform? It was just for now. As soon as Mum got a better job we'd move somewhere bigger and I'd get new clothes.

Chadwick was waiting for us by the school gates with Bates and Wilson. I didn't see him at first, but I knew he was there because Neil's face suddenly went all funny. We were in the middle of an argument about penalties and I knew something was wrong. Then I heard Chadwick shout.

"Hey, the piece of scum has got a school uniform!" he yelled. Bates and Wilson laughed.

I know I should have felt embarrassed, or even scared, but I didn't. For some reason, I wasn't scared today. In fact I felt so good that I walked right over to him.

"Say that again, moron!" I told him.

Chadwick blinked at me. I don't think anyone had ever stood up to him before, and it took him by surprise. Behind him, Bates and Wilson both let out a "Whoo!" that made him focus on me again.

"What did you just call me?" he grunted.

I took a deep breath. How come I was this brave all of a sudden? I wanted to stick with it while it lasted. "Are you deaf as well as ugly?" I asked. "I called you a moron!"

I turned back to see Neil. He looked like he was about to wet himself.

The split-second I wasn't looking at Chadwick was enough time for him to grab me. He got my new school tie in his fist – sorry, my second-hand school tie – and dragged me towards him. My nose was almost touching his and I could smell his rotten breath.

"No one speaks to me like that and gets away with it!" he growled.

"Just as well I'm not 'no one' then, isn't it?" I yelled. Before I even knew I was doing it, I swung my arm back and slammed my fist into his belly. He groaned and bent over – all the breath knocked out of him.

I couldn't believe I'd done it. I'd never hit anyone before – ever! But it felt good. Well, not good, exactly, but just right. At last I was paying everyone back for all my problems. It

felt like I was hitting the men who'd come and taken my Wii away because my mum had missed so many payments. Like I was hitting the people next door to our new flat who played music until two in the morning when my mum had to get up early for work.

It felt like I was hitting my dad.

I rammed my knee into Chadwick's nose. He gave a soft "Oof!" and blood spurted over my school trousers.

Then all hell let loose.

Chapter 4
A Really Good Day

Ian Bates jumped on top of me but I got my fist on his chin first. He spun round, stunned, and then fell back on the metal school gate. I grabbed the back of his school jumper and pulled him to the floor where he curled up into a little ball. He looked like he was trying not to cry.

Then I turned to Billy Wilson, who was slowly backing away with his hands up in front of him. For one second, I actually felt sorry for him. Bates and Wilson had never had anyone act this way towards them – not since they'd started hanging round with Chadwick anyway. They'd never had to fight their own battles. I stopped feeling sorry for Billy Wilson and I took a step forward.

"Please don't hurt me!" Wilson began, then he turned and ran away. Bates got up slowly and ran after him.

That just left Chadwick. He was still bent over double and holding his bloody nose. I grabbed the back of his hair and lifted his head up. His eyes were wide open and he looked terrified.

"Never come near me again!" I growled.

"I'll get you for this!" he gulped.

I pulled his hair hard so it hurt. "No, you won't!" I snarled and I pushed him away. Chadwick's face had blood all over it. He got

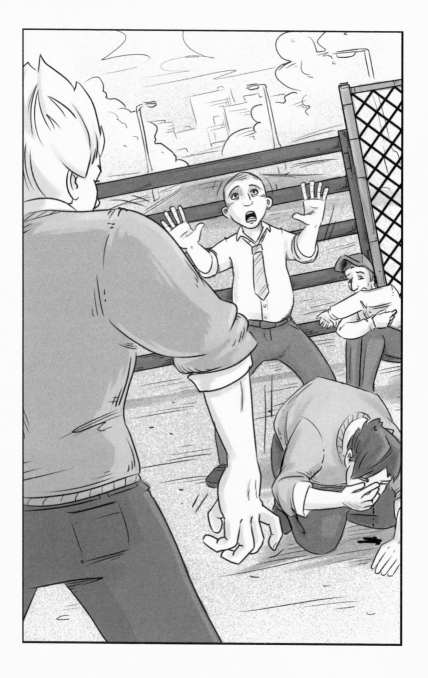

up and ran off. I knew I wouldn't be getting any more trouble from him and his mates.

I turned back to Neil and laughed. He had a new look on his face – one I'd not seen before. His chin was nearly touching his shoes. In fact, everyone coming into school had stopped to watch what I'd just done. They were all staring at me.

"Where did you learn to do that?" Neil asked.

I gave a shrug. "Dunno," I had to say. "I suppose I'm just fed up of being picked on all the time." I grabbed my bag and started to walk into school with Neil.

"You were like something out of a Kung Fu movie!" he grinned.

"I wasn't that good!" I said. But I have to admit, I felt pretty proud that I'd stood up for myself at last. And I did like the way everyone else in the yard was staring at me. I guess in a way I'd stopped Steven Chadwick from bullying them too.

At the door into the school block there were two Year Sevens swapping their latest football stickers.

"Out of my way!" I snarled. The kids grabbed their stickers and ran.

Neil froze. "What did you do that for?" he asked.

"Do what?" I didn't understand.

"You told those kids to get out of your way."

"No, I didn't," I said and I opened the door. "Now, hurry up. If we're late for Maths, we'll never hear the end of it."

"Matthew Miller!" The voice bellowed along the corridor and I looked up to see Mr Green, the English teacher. Steven Chadwick was behind him with a fist full of wet paper towels pressed against his nose.

The teacher stopped in front of me. "Did you do this?" he asked.

Chadwick's eyes were red with tears. I couldn't believe it – the coward had gone running to a teacher the very first time someone had hit him back!

"Do what, sir?" I asked.

Mr Green's face was red with anger. "Did you do this to Steven Chadwick?" he asked.

I looked at him as if I just didn't know what he meant. "No, it wasn't me, sir," I lied. "When I got to the school gates there were two bullies picking on Steven – Ian Bates and

Billy Wilson I think they're called. I ran to try and help him, but I couldn't pull them off."

"Is this true?" asked the teacher.

"Yes, sir!" I nodded. "I suppose Steven must have seen me running to help him and then he thought I was one of the bullies." I gave Chadwick a look to tell him he'd be in deep trouble if he ever dared to disagree with me. He sniffed and looked away. He didn't say a word.

"Neil was with me, sir," I went on. "He'll tell you it wasn't me."

Mr Green turned to Neil. "Is this correct?" he growled. "Is that the truth?"

Neil gulped hard. He looked scared, but I knew he'd stand up for me. He was my friend, after all. "Yes, sir," he said, in the end.

"Very well," said Mr Green. "Now, get along to your first lesson, both of you."

I strode away along the corridor. This was turning into a really good day.

Chapter 5
New Rules

Steven Chadwick wasn't in school for the next few days. I expect he was embarrassed that it was him that had got beaten up for once. If he had any sense, he'd know it was a good idea to stay away from me, and I didn't blame him. Since I'd stood up for myself against the bullies, I felt better than I had for ages.

Other kids were starting to show me some respect, as well. If anyone got in my way, or did something I didn't like, all I had to do was warn them and they'd scurry off.

It's amazing the difference it makes when you start to act cool. Now, I could always get a game of football at break time. The kids in my year never let me play when I'd first started at the school. And the boys in charge of the tuck shop suddenly started to give me too much change when I went to buy a packet of crisps. Ever since I'd broken Chadwick's nose, I was making money!

Neil was with me all the time. He knew he wouldn't be picked on so long as he was my friend. I even learned to put up with his stupid faces – like the one he made when I didn't want to wait in the queue at lunchtime.

"Why did you push your way to the front?" he asked, his face twisted up. He

looked like a baby who needed his nappy changing.

"I didn't push my way anywhere," I pointed out. "The others let me go ahead of them."

"Yeah," he muttered, "because they're all scared of you."

I spun round so I was looking right at him. "What did you say?" I asked.

I stared at Neil and, for a second, a flash of fear flicked across his face. What an idiot! He's my mate, and I'd never do anything to hurt him. So long as he did what he was told, of course.

"I just think ..." he started to say

I didn't let him finish. "Come on," I said. "Let's go and get a game of football in before the bell goes."

Neil didn't meet me at the school gates that night. Maybe he'd got a tummy ache and gone crying to the school nurse or something.

I was about half way home when I spotted some kids from the year below me on the other side of the road. They were looking at me and whispering. Then, one of them laughed.

I felt anger bubble up inside me and I ran across the street. I made a rude face at the driver of the car who was honking me.

I marched up to the smaller of the two kids and gave him a push. "What's so funny?" I asked.

"What?" he squeaked.

"I said, what's so funny?"

"Nothing!" said the kid. "We weren't even looking at you!"

"Liar!" I pushed him again. There was no way I was going to put up with that sort of attitude. Then his mate decided to be a hero …

"Leave him alone!" he shouted and he stepped out in front of me and put a hand on my chest. He pushed me away from his friend.

It only took me a couple of punches and I'd knocked him to the ground. He lay there moaning. Honestly – some people just don't even try to fight back!

"Matthew?" someone said. Neil was standing just behind me, watching.

"There you are!" I grinned, leaving the two Year Sevens to grow up and sort themselves out. "I thought I'd missed you tonight."

Neil was watching the two kids as they raced away. "What's going on?" he asked.

"Nothing I can't handle," I told him.

Neil took a deep breath. "You've changed," he said.

"What are you talking about?" I asked.

"You're not the same person any more," he said. "Ever since you had that fight with Chadwick, you're getting ... well – you're turning into a bully yourself!"

"Don't be silly!" I said.

"No, I mean it, Matthew ..."

I didn't let him finish. "Actually," I said, "I've been thinking. I don't think Matthew's a good name for me anymore."

Neil made a puzzled face. It wasn't pretty. "You don't?" he asked.

"No," I said, and I put my arm around his shoulders. "It's too – I dunno – too wimpy. From now on, I'd like you to call me Matt The Man!"

Chapter 6
All Change

My mum didn't look very happy as she opened the door for me when I got home and, when I looked into the living room, I knew why. Mr Green, the English teacher, was there.

"What do you want?" I asked him.

"Matthew!" my mum snapped. "Don't you dare talk to your teacher like that!"

"Well, he's been on my back for days!" I moaned. "I've had enough of him."

"I'm afraid Matthew's attitude is why I'm here, Mrs Miller," said Green.

"Oh, shut up!" I sneered.

"Go to your room and get changed, now!" ordered my mum.

I stomped off, muttering insults softly to myself. What right did that idiot have to stick his nose into my home life? I had enough of him at school!

I took off my jumper.

Why was he on my back all the time? I'd only just got rid of Chadwick and his monkeys. I didn't need someone else bugging me.

I dropped my shirt and tie on the bed and pulled on a T-shirt.

I knew he was only checking I was OK, but my mum had enough to do without having to worry about how I was getting on at school. It wasn't fair.

I kicked my school trousers off and put on my jeans.

I didn't want to give anyone any trouble. He might be strict, but Mr Green was OK, as teachers go.

"I'm sorry, Mr Green," I said when I went back into the living room. "I shouldn't have talked to you that way."

Mr Green looked surprised. "Thank you, Matthew," he said. "What a nice change around – and more like the lad who first arrived at Elm Road."

I nodded. "Things have just been getting on top of me lately. It won't happen again." I stood. "Now – who'd like a cup of tea?"

I told Neil about Mr Green's visit as we got dressed after PE the following day.

"I know you don't want to come home after a hard day in school and find a teacher sitting there, but it felt good to have a man in the house again," I said. "It's just been me and Mum since my dad left."

"Hey, you never know," grinned Neil as I pulled on my school trousers, "he and your mum might hit it off!"

"Don't say that," I sneered. "I'd never get away without doing my homework if he was around all the time!"

"Yeah, but he'd have all the answers at home," said Neil, while I buttoned my shirt.

"A few peeks inside his briefcase, and you'd never fail an exam ever again."

"Life's not all about exams!" I snapped. "You're such a geek sometimes!"

I lifted my collar and began to do up my tie, but Neil still wouldn't leave it. "Alright," he moaned. "Stay cool!" I pulled my jumper over my head. God, he was beginning to annoy me. "I was only saying that your mum must be pretty lonely since your dad left ..." Neil began again.

I grabbed Neil's shirt and pushed him back against the wall, my face right up against his. "Green will never get anywhere near my mum!" I roared. "Do you hear?"

"Y-yes!" Neil stammered. "But, Matthew ..."

"It's not Matthew," I bellowed. "It's Matt The Man to you!" I couldn't believe how angry I was. "And if I ever catch Green near our flat again, I'll kill him! I'm beginning to think Chadwick's brother had the right idea!

That's when Neil saw the label on my school jumper. "DTM!" he blurted out.

I gripped his shirt even harder. "What?" I shouted. The other kids grabbed their bags and dashed out of the changing room, leaving me and Neil alone.

"DTM!" he squeaked. "Dan The Man! Your uniform used to belong to Chadwick's brother!"

"So? What if my uniform did used to belong to Daniel Chadwick?" I snarled. "Are you having a go at me for wearing second-hand clothes?"

"No!" Neil pulled away from my grip and rubbed at his throat. "Don't you get it?" he said. "Ever since you've been wearing that uniform you've been different."

"I've stood up for myself, if that's what you mean," I said.

"It's more than that, Matthew," Neil went on. "You've started to be a bully yourself. It's like ... like the uniform is possessing you!"

Chapter 7
When Push Comes to Shove

I looked hard at Neil for a long time. "Don't be so stupid!" I shouted. "How can a school uniform possess someone?"

"I don't know!" said Neil. "But since PE you've been getting angrier and angrier – ever since you started putting on those clothes!"

"You're making it up!" I shouted. "I haven't changed at all."

"Oh, no?" said Neil. "Then tell me how you feel about Mr Green sat alone with your mum before you got home last night? What were they getting up to?"

I forced Neil against the wall again. "Nothing happened!" I spat in his face. "And I'll make sure it never can!"

I grabbed my bag and stormed off. I kicked open the door to the changing rooms. I knew what I had to do.

I found Mr Green in an empty classroom. He was marking some books. "Ah, Matthew," he said as I stopped in the doorway. "Tell your mum thanks for last night. I really enjoyed myself!"

I was across the classroom in a second, my hands clawing for his throat. "Why?" I roared. "What happened? What did you do to her?"

"Nothing!" Mr Green began. "We just talked about music!"

"Music?" I asked. I grabbed Mr Green's hair and slammed him back against the wall. "What music?"

The teacher looked scared now. "We like the same bands!" he said. "That's all. We thought we might go to a gig togeth– "

"No!" I screamed, and I pressed him harder against the wall. "You're going nowhere with her!"

"Matthew, stop it!" someone shouted from the classroom door. I looked round. Neil was standing there. This time, his face wasn't twisted up at all. "Jeez, man!" he said. "You look like a wild animal!"

"Get lost, Neil!" I shouted. "This has got nothing to do with you!"

"It has!" Neil yelled back. "This is the classroom where it happened, Matthew. This is the classroom where Daniel Chadwick killed a teacher!"

I turned back and stared into Mr Green's terrified eyes. "Then I've come to the right place!"

I kicked a desk out of my way. "I've had enough of other people screwing up my life!"

I roared. I grabbed Mr Green's jacket. He tried to pull away from me.

"Don't do this, Matthew!" Neil shouted. "This isn't you! It's that uniform making you act like this!"

"Get out of here," I snarled, "or you'll be next!"

Neil didn't leave. In fact, he stepped up closer to me. "OK," said. "I'm next. But first – prove me wrong! Take off that uniform and see if you still feel the same way. If you do, you can kill both Mr Green and me!"

Mr Green stood up. "Matthew," he began.

"Quiet, you!" I barked. "Suit yourself," I growled at Neil. "At least this way I won't get your blood on my shirt!"

I didn't look away from Neil as I pulled off my jumper. What an idiot to even think that all this was down to a stupid school uniform.

The shirt and tie came next. I blinked and looked away. For a second, I wasn't sure why I was angry with Neil any more. But then I remembered he'd stood up to me. Now I was going to prove that he was wrong about the uniform.

As I stepped out of my trousers, I felt like a massive load had been lifted off my back. I looked at Neil and Mr Green. They both looked scared. No – they looked terrified ... *of me*! What had I done?

"I'm sorry!" I whispered. "So sorry!"

Mr Green hurried over and helped me into a chair. As I sat down, I kicked the school uniform as far away from me as I could. It was over. The uniform had made me feel really powerful but now I wanted to be

the real me again. I didn't even care if I got
bullied. I put my head in my hands and
started to cry.

If I had looked up that point, I'd have seen
Neil picking up the different bits of the
uniform and stuffing them into his bag ...